This Book Belongs To

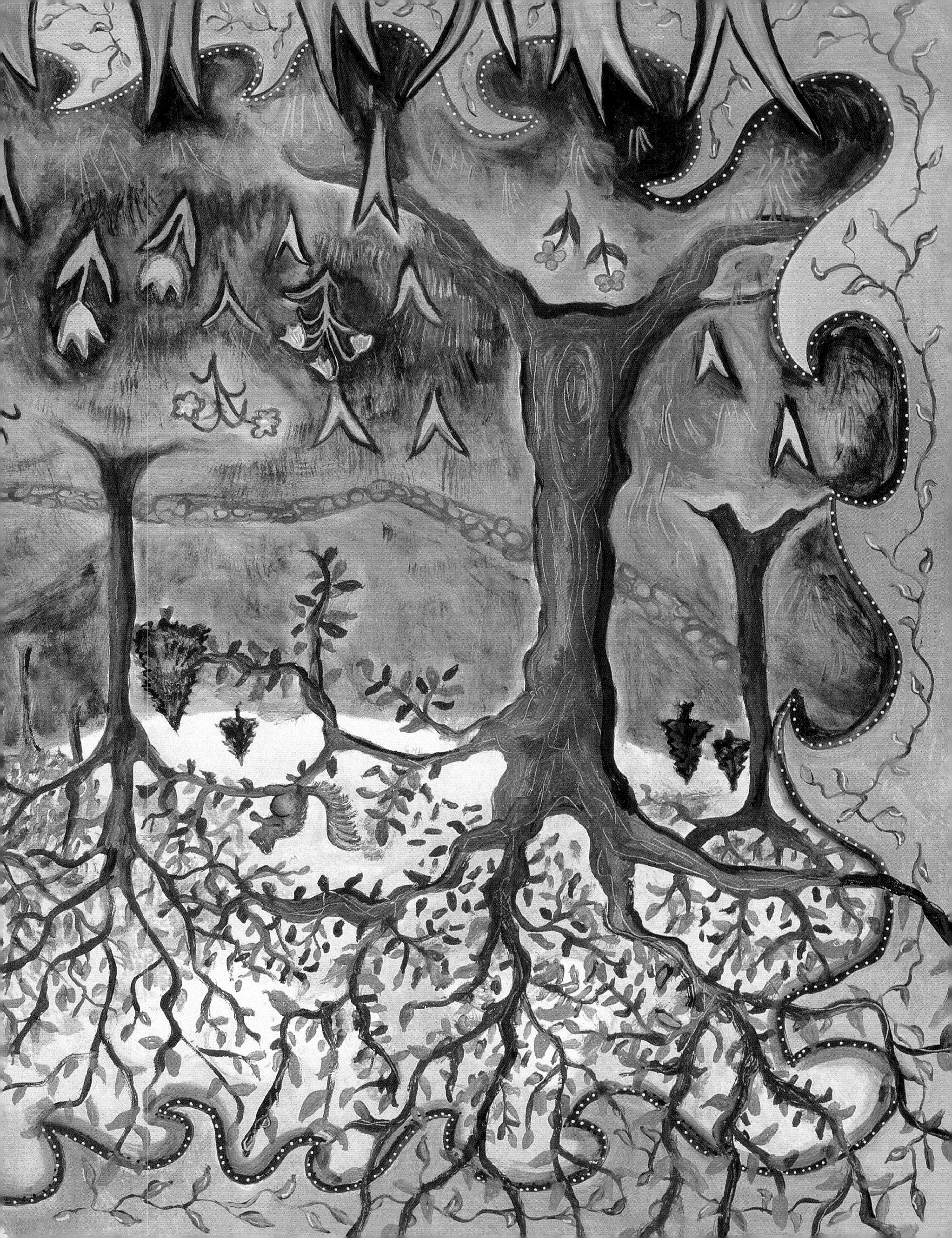

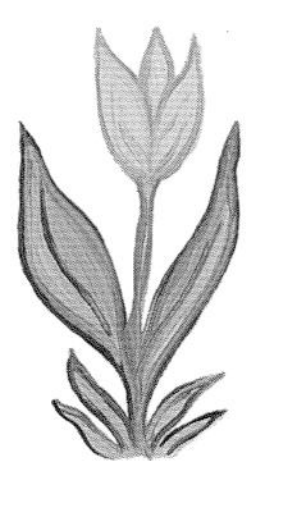

Thank you to my good friend Randy Milgrom
for his help in refining my manuscript for this book.

Printed in China

9 8 7 6 5 4 3 2 1
Digit on the right indicates the number of this printing

Library of Congress Cataloging-in-Publication Number 2002108139

ISBN 0-7624-1491-X

Designed by Gwen Galeone
Edited by Susan K. Hom
Typography: Jacoby and Century Old Style

This book may be ordered by mail from the publisher.
But try your bookstore first!

Published by Courage Books, an imprint of
Running Press Book Publishers
125 South Twenty-second Street
Philadelphia, Pennsylvania 19103-4399

Visit us on the web!
www.runningpress.com

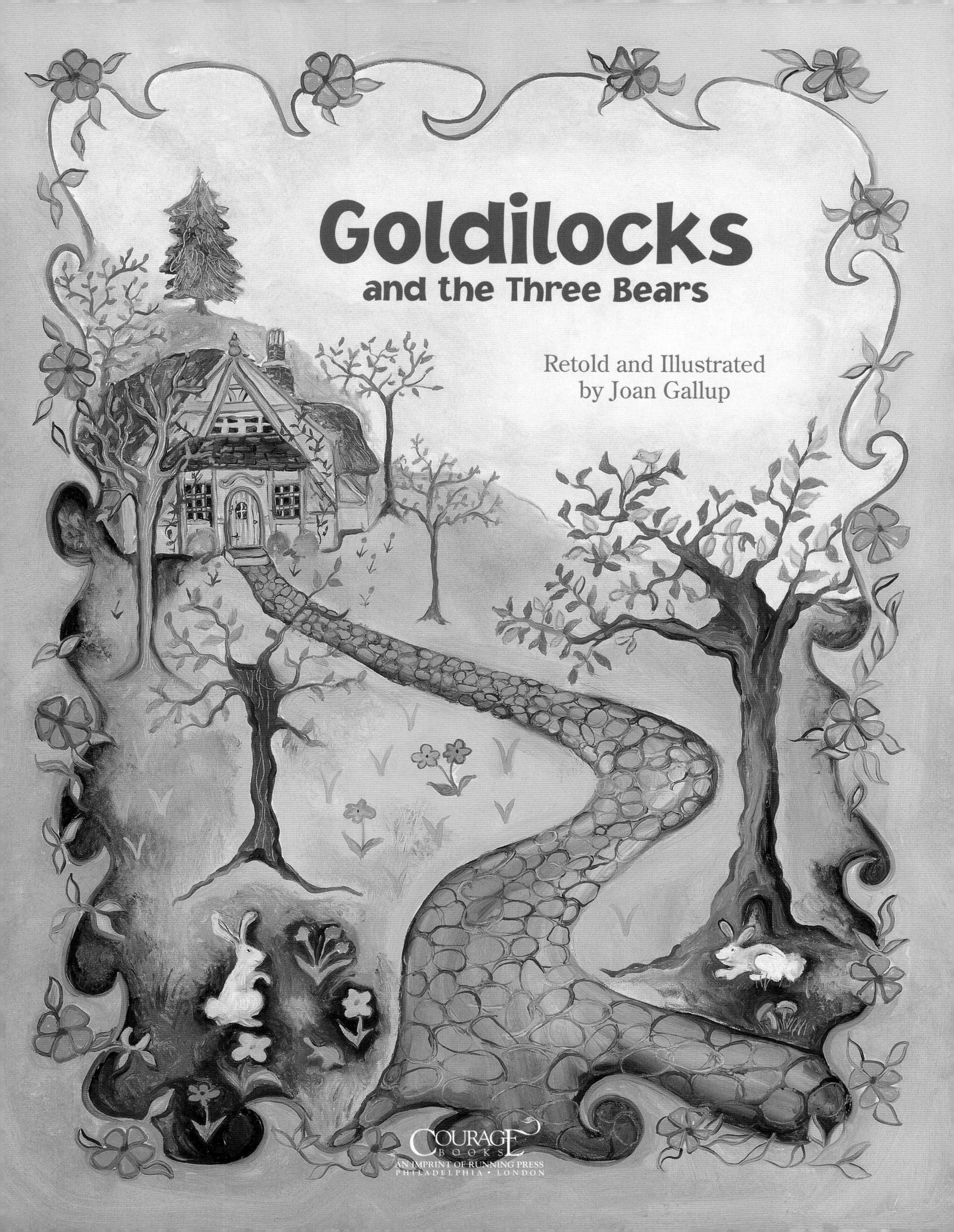
Goldilocks
and the Three Bears
Retold and Illustrated
by Joan Gallup
COURAGE
BOOKS
AN IMPRINT OF RUNNING PRESS
PHILADELPHIA • LONDON

Papa Bear, Mama Bear, and Baby Bear lived in a little cottage deep in the forest. One morning, Mama Bear was serving breakfast. She poured porridge from a steaming pot into Papa Bear's bowl, then her own bowl, and then into Baby Bear's bowl.

"Mama, this porridge is too hot!" cried Baby Bear, holding his spoon mid-air.

"Yes, indeed," said Mama. "We must go for a walk while our porridge cools."

The Bear family headed out for a walk.

Outside the forest, on the edge of the village, lived little Goldilocks.

"Goldilocks," said her mother. "Please go into the woods and pick some flowers." So Goldilocks gathered her basket and started down the path.

"But don't go too far, and don't get lost, and watch out for wild animals!" her mother quickly called after her.

Goldilocks followed the path through the woods. She walked and walked until she came upon a pretty patch of blue and white flowers. She knelt, smelled them, and placed a few in her basket.

Further down the path, Goldilocks found a patch of bright yellow flowers. She placed them in her basket too.

Then she hurried on her way, running off the path to gather some pretty pink flowers, which she spotted just ahead.

Suddenly Goldilocks looked about. Where was the path? "I think I'm lost," she thought.

In the distance, she saw a small cottage with tinted glass windows and pretty vines growing up its sides.

Goldilocks went to the cottage. She knocked on the door, but there was no answer. Goldilocks tried the knob. The door opened. "I'll just step inside," she thought.

Once inside, Goldilocks smelled something wonderful.
"Mmmmm . . . porridge with hot brown sugar!" she said.

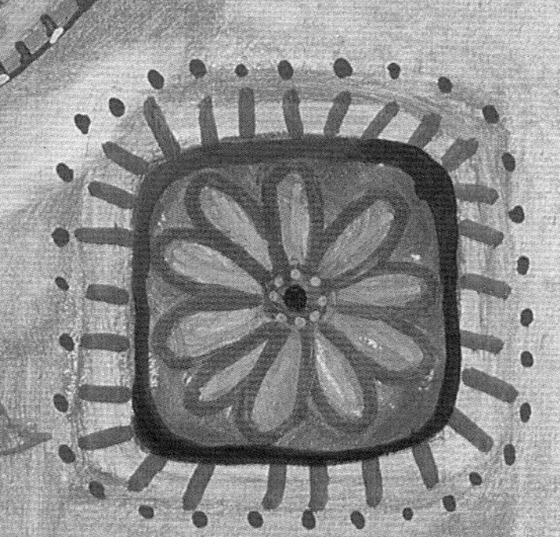

Three bowls filled with porridge sat on a table in the kitchen. There was one great big bowl, one medium-sized bowl, and one itsy-bitsy, baby-sized bowl. “No one will mind if I just taste a little,” Goldilocks thought.

So she tried the great big bowl with the great big spoon. “Oh! Too hot!” she cried.

Then Goldilocks tried the medium-sized bowl, with the medium-sized spoon. “Ugh! Too cold!” she blurted.

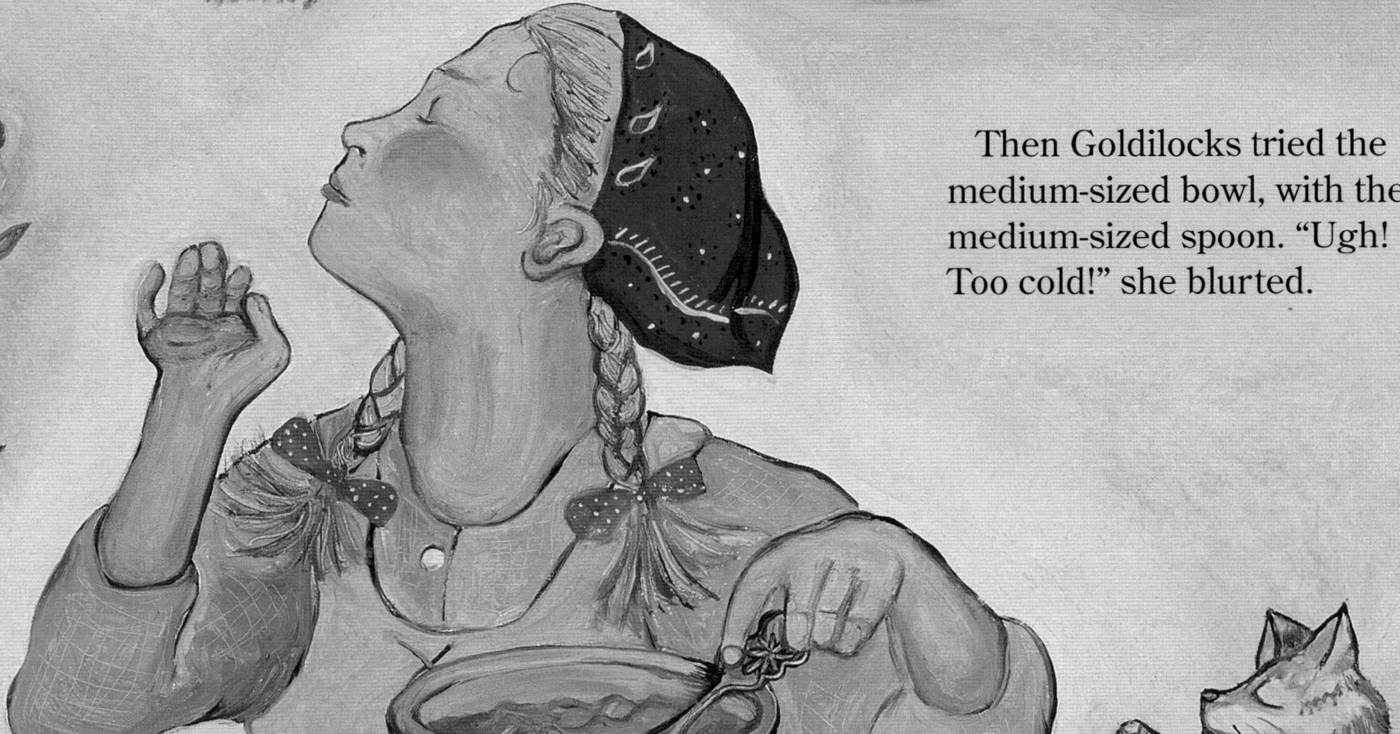

Finally there was the itsy-bitsy, baby-sized bowl with the tiny spoon, which Goldilocks picked up. She tasted the porridge. “Not too hot, not too cold. This porridge is just right!” she said. And she ate it all up!

“I’m so full, I must sit down,” said Goldilocks.

In the next room, there were three chairs for sitting: one great big wooden chair, one medium-sized cushioned chair, and one itsy-bitsy, baby-sized chair.

Goldilocks tried the great big chair first. She climbed up high to get into it.
When she sat down, her feet wouldn't touch the ground!
"Much too big, and stiff too!" she exclaimed.

Next Goldilocks climbed into the medium-sized chair. It looked comfortable, but Goldilocks immediately sank too far into the fluff of the cushions.

"Much too soft," she complained, as she struggled out of the chair.

Last was the itsy-bitsy, baby-sized chair. Goldilocks sat down. Her feet touched the floor, and she did not sink down. "This chair is just right!" said Goldilocks gleefully.

But suddenly the chair gave way, breaking into pieces! Goldilocks fell to the ground with a thud! "Oh dear!" said Goldilocks.

Now Goldilocks was feeling drowsy. “I must lie down,” she thought. “No one will mind if I just rest a bit.” So Goldilocks walked to the bedroom.

Inside she saw three beds, all in a row: one great big bed, one medium-sized bed, and one itsy-bitsy, baby-sized bed.

Goldilocks climbed into the great big bed, lay on its great big, hard mattress, and felt very uncomfortable.

"This bed is much too big!" she said.

Goldilocks moved into the medium-sized bed. Now she sank into the soft mattress, with its many pillows and quilts, and nearly got lost.

"Much too soft!" she cried.

Goldilocks climbed into the itsy-bitsy, baby-sized bed. Not too hard, not too big. Not too soft, not too squishy. And just the right size. "This bed is just right!" she cried.

Goldilocks fell fast asleep.

Meanwhile, the three bears were heading home, having finished their morning walk.

“We shall have our porridge, our porridge, our porridge!” sang Baby Bear all the way home.

The Bear family arrived at their cottage. "Why is the door wide open, Papa?" asked Baby Bear. "The wind must have been blowing," said Papa Bear.

“Come, we will eat our porridge,” said Mama Bear, as they headed toward the kitchen.

The Bear family sat down.
“Someone has been into my
porridge!” exclaimed Papa Bear.

"Someone has been tasting mine, too!" said Mama Bear.

"Someone has been into my porridge," said Baby Bear, "and they've eaten it all up!" Baby Bear gazed wide-eyed into his empty bowl.

The bears headed toward the sitting room.

"Someone has been sitting in my chair!" said Papa Bear.

“Someone has been sitting in my chair, too,” said Mama Bear,
“and my cushions are all a mess!”

“Someone has been sitting in my chair,” cried Baby Bear, “and it is broken all to bits!”

All three bears now tiptoed toward the bedroom. In walked Papa Bear, then Mama Bear, and last of all, Baby Bear.

"Someone has been in my bed!" growled Papa Bear. He frowned at the yellow flower lying on his bed.

"Someone has been in mine also," wailed Mama Bear. She shook her head at her favorite pillows, which had been moved.

"Someone has been in my bed too, and there she is!" shouted Baby Bear.

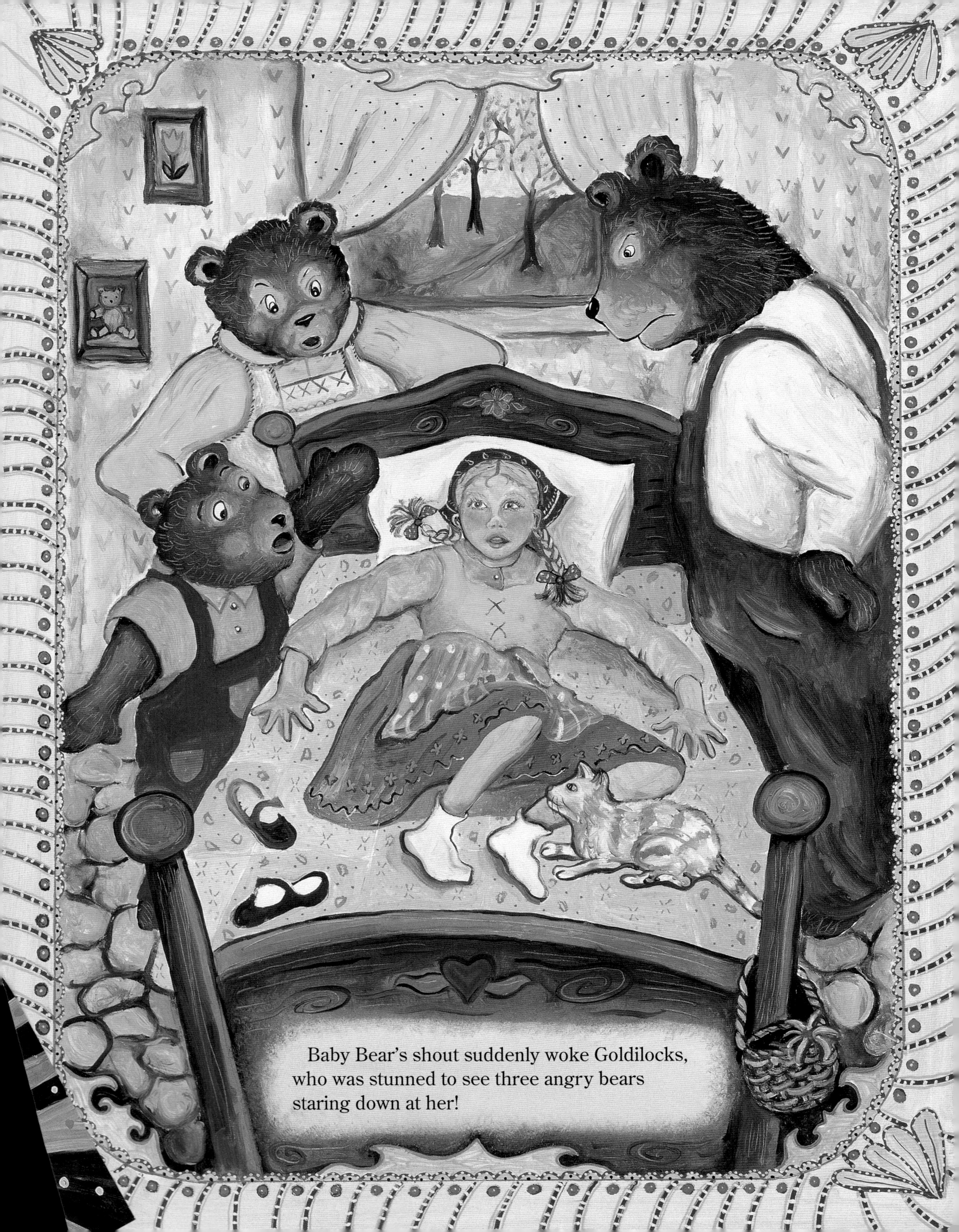

Baby Bear's shout suddenly woke Goldilocks, who was stunned to see three angry bears staring down at her!

Goldilocks jumped up out of the bed and bolted out the door!

And she ran and ran, all the way home,
never to be seen by the Bear family again!